Sports Build Character

TRUSTWORTHINESS IN SPORTS

by Todd Kortemeier

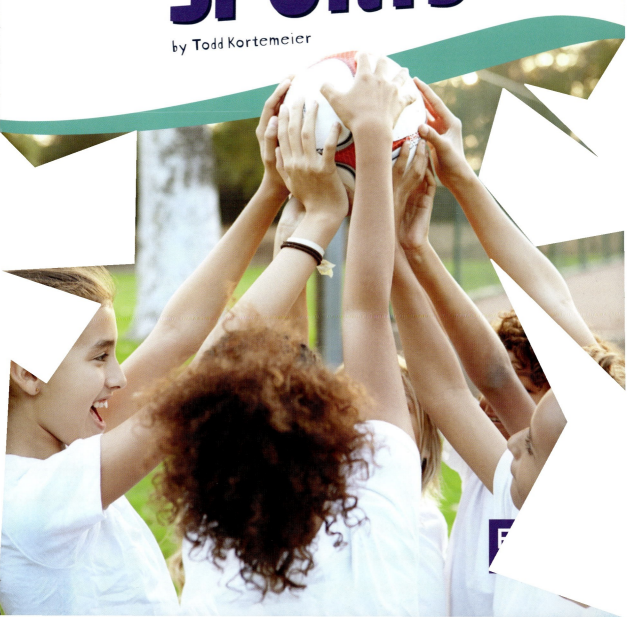

www.focusreaders.com

Focus Readers is distributed by North Star Editions:
sales@northstareditions.com | 888-417-0195

Produced for Focus Readers by Red Line Editorial.

Photographs ©: bowdenimages/iStockphoto, cover, 1; bmcent1/iStockphoto, 4–5; Rawpixel.com/Shutterstock Images, 6; Olga Besnard/Shutterstock Images, 8–9, 29; Markku Ulander/Rex Features/AP Images, 10; Richard Paul Kane/Shutterstock Images, 12; Brody Schmidt/AP Images, 15; Matt Slocum/AP Images, 16; Brandon Dill/AP Images, 18; Fred Kfoury III/Icon Sportswire/AP Images, 20; PeopleImages/iStockphoto, 22–23; asiseeit/iStockphoto, 24; ideabug/iStockphoto, 26–27

ISBN
978-1-63517-536-3 (hardcover)
978-1-63517-608-7 (paperback)
978-1-63517-752-7 (ebook pdf)
978-1-63517-680-3 (hosted ebook)

Library of Congress Control Number: 2017948107

Printed in the United States of America
Mankato, MN
November, 2017

About the Author

Todd Kortemeier is a writer and editor from Minneapolis. He has written more than 50 books for young people, primarily on sports topics.

TABLE OF CONTENTS

CHAPTER 1

WHAT IS TRUSTWORTHINESS?

Everyone wants someone they can count on. This person could be a friend, teacher, or family member. Life can be hard. It is easier with people to rely on for help. People like this are trustworthy.

 Rock climbers trust their partner to not let them fall.

 Athletes show trust by following instructions from their coach.

Trustworthy people do not lie or **cheat**. They admit when they are wrong. And they do what they say they are going to do.

Trust is important in sports. Teammates need to know they can count on one another. Coaches want to know their players are up to the job. Trust does not always come easy. It must be earned over time. But the result is worth it. Teammates who trust one another know how to work together.

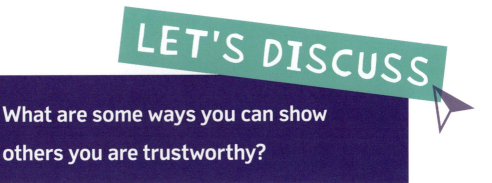

LET'S DISCUSS

What are some ways you can show others you are trustworthy?

CHAPTER 2

TRUSTWORTHINESS IN ACTION

Like all sports, **pairs** figure skating takes teamwork, skill, and strength. It also takes trust. Figure skating often requires one partner to toss the other partner into the air.

In a star lift, one partner lifts the other with just one arm.

 Maia and Alex Shibutani won bronze medals in the 2017 World Championships.

All it takes is a small mistake for a skater to get hurt.

There is also the danger of the skaters' **blades**. One wrong move could cause a skater to collide with the other's blades.

Maia and Alex Shibutani compete in ice dancing. Ice dancers do not perform jumps. But these Olympians have to trust each other just as much to succeed. They practice for many hours. This gives each skater confidence to do their best. They know they are there for each other, win or lose.

LET'S DISCUSS

What are some ways figure skaters might build trust?

Football coaches trust defenders to keep their heads in the game.

A football team's defense is based on trust. There are several lines of defense that players must break through. If a player gets through a line, more defenders must be there to make the stop. Defenders trust one another to be ready.

Oklahoma State's Brodrick Brown and Shaun Lewis trusted each other in a 2010 game. They were playing their biggest **rival**, the Oklahoma Sooners. It was a close game. The lead changed hands several times.

In the game's second quarter, Sooners **quarterback** Landry Jones threw a pass toward the **sideline**.

But the pass was too high for his team's receivers. Brown was tracking the ball. He jumped up to make the **interception**.

Brown got his hands on the ball. But there was no way he could stay in bounds. That was when Lewis arrived. Brown swatted the ball toward Lewis. Lewis made the catch. Then he returned the ball to Sooners territory. It was one of the best plays of the year.

 Lewis scored a touchdown earlier in the 2010 game against the Sooners.

 In 2013, James became the youngest NBA player to score 20,000 points.

Few basketball players can match the achievements of LeBron James.

He made the All-Star team in 13 out of his first 14 seasons. In that time, he won three championships.

In 2015, James drew attention for calling plays during games. Usually, only a team's coach calls plays. But James's coach trusted him to do it. James's previous coaches trusted him, too. Before the Cleveland Cavaliers, James called plays with the Miami Heat. He called plays in every game after his **rookie** season.

 James calls to his teammates during an October 2015 game.

Oftentimes, James could sense

how a game was going. He would

call a play to take advantage of the situation. Other times, he stuck to the team's original plan. James's teammates and coaches trusted him to make these important decisions. The coach was still the team's leader. But James was the leader on the court.

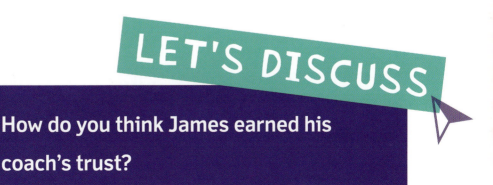

LET'S DISCUSS

How do you think James earned his coach's trust?

 Spieth (front) hugs caddie Michael Greller after a 2017 championship win.

Golf is an individual sport. Still, the golfer is not alone on the course. Pro golfers have caddies to help them. A caddie's job is to carry the golfer's clubs. But in reality, caddies do much more.

When Jordan Spieth turned pro in 2012, he hired Michael Greller as his caddie. Spieth and Greller are a team. Greller gives Spieth advice during tournaments. Sometimes, the two disagree. Every time they disagree, Spieth and Greller learn more about each other. This helps them build trust.

LET'S DISCUSS

If you were a golfer, who would you pick as your caddie? Why?

CHAPTER 3

TRUSTWORTHINESS AND YOU

People show trustworthiness through their actions. When your actions help others, you build trust. When your actions hurt others, you lose their trust.

Teammates trust one another to not give up.

Family members build trust by helping one another at home.

Once trust is lost, it can be hard to replace.

Everyone has the power to trust others. When you trust someone, you have confidence in his or her abilities. Teammates who trust each other become better players. They believe in one another's ability to play the game. Trust helps players make difficult plays.

Trust is important off the field as well. Good friends are honest and dependable. They show up when you need them. That's what friends are for. With time, trust helps friendships grow stronger.

LET'S DISCUSS

What would you do if a close friend lied to you?

ARE YOU TRUSTWORTHY?

Ask yourself these questions and decide.

- Am I honest?
- Do I play and act fairly?
- Do I follow through on promises?
- Do I work hard?
- Can people depend on me?

Everyone likes to be trusted. Think of the one person you trust most. This week, challenge yourself to thank that person. You could make the person a card. Or you could do something kind.

Trustworthy friends always have your back.

FOCUS ON
TRUSTWORTHINESS

Write your answers on a separate piece of paper.

1. Write a sentence summarizing how Shaun Lewis showed trustworthiness in Chapter 2.

2. Would you want to try pairs figure skating? Why or why not?

3. Who did Jordan Spieth hire as his caddie?
   A. LeBron James
   B. Alex Shibutani
   C. Michael Greller

4. What would have happened if Shaun Lewis had not caught the interception?
   A. Oklahoma would have kept the ball.
   B. The game would have ended.
   C. Lewis would have had a penalty called on him.

5. What does **achievements** mean in this book?

Few basketball players can match the achievements of LeBron James. He made the All-Star team in 13 out of his first 14 seasons.

    A. successes

    B. challenges

    C. losses

6. What does **tracking** mean in this book?

Brown was tracking the ball. He jumped up to make the interception.

    A. holding

    B. watching

    C. ignoring

Answer key on page 32.

GLOSSARY

blades
Sharp metal edges on the bottom of ice skates.

cheat
To break the rules on purpose to gain an advantage.

interception
A play in which the defense catches a pass, gaining possession of the ball.

pairs
A form of figure skating in which two people skate together.

quarterback
An offensive football player responsible for throwing passes.

rival
A team or player that has an intense and ongoing competition against another team or player.

rookie
A professional athlete in his or her first year.

sideline
The area to the sides of a football field, where playing does not occur.

TO LEARN MORE

BOOKS

Nelson, Robin. *Am I a Good Friend? A Book About Trustworthiness.* Minneapolis: Lerner Publications, 2014.

Raatma, Lucia. *Trustworthiness.* Ann Arbor, MI: Cherry Lake Publishing, 2014.

Vermond, Kira. *Half-Truths and Brazen Lies: An Honest Look at Lying.* Berkeley: Owlkids Books, 2016.

NOTE TO EDUCATORS

Visit **www.focusreaders.com** to find lesson plans, activities, links, and other resources related to this title.

INDEX

A
All-Star, 17

B
Brown, Brodrick, 13–14

C
caddie, 20–21
Cleveland Cavaliers, 17

G
Greller, Michael, 21

I
ice dancing, 11

J
James, LeBron, 16–19
Jones, Landry, 13

L
Lewis, Shaun, 13–14

M
Miami Heat, 17

O
Oklahoma Sooners, 13–14
Oklahoma State, 13

S
Shibutani, Alex, 11
Shibutani, Maia, 11
Spieth, Jordan, 21

All About Canadian Communities

The All About Series

Towns

Maryrose O'Neill

THOMSON
★
NELSON

Canada

Australia   Canada   Mexico   Singapore   Spain   United Kingdom   United States

THOMSON
★
NELSON ™

All About Canadian Communities: Towns
Maryrose O'Neill

Series Concept
Barb McDermott
Gail McKeown

Director of Publishing
David Steele

Publisher
Carol Stokes

Executive Managing Editor, Development
Cheryl Turner

Executive Managing Editor, Production
Nicola Balfour

Copyright © 2003 by Nelson, a division of Thomson Canada Limited.

Printed and bound in Canada
1 2 3 4 06 05 04 03

For more information contact Nelson,
1120 Birchmount Road, Toronto, Ontario, M1K 5G4.
Or you can visit our Internet site at
http://www.nelson.com

Cover: Canmore, Alberta

Program Managers
Leah-Ann Lymer
Laura Edlund

Developmental Editor
Martha Ayim

Senior Production Editor
Karin Fediw

Copy Editor
Susan Till

Composition and Cover Design
Erich Falkenberg and Suzanne Peden

Photo Credits: Cover: Adrian Wyld/CP Picture Archive; Page 3: Victor Last/Geographical Visual Aids; Page 7: Barrett & MacKay Photography; Page 11: R. Hartmier/ First Light; Page 13: © Lowell Georgia/Corbis/Magma; Page 15: Canadian Science and Technology Museum/ CN Collection, Image # CN003374; Page 17: Courtesy of Town of Nackawic; Page 19: Barrett & MacKay Photography; Page 23: ASTROLab du Mont-Mégantic; Page 25: Frances Ezinga Photography; page 27: Barrett & MacKay Photography; Page 29: Al Harvey/The Slide Farm.

Illustrations: Deborah Crowle and Andrew Breithaupt

Production Coordinator
Ferial Suleman

Permissions/Photo Research
Vicki Gould

Printer
Transcontinental Printing Inc.

Reviewers
Nancy Bullock, Wainwright, Alberta
Margaret Bennett, Wainwright, Alberta
Bruce Murphy, Amherst, Nova Scotia
Geneviève Maheux, Lac-Mégantic, Quebec

National Library of Canada Cataloguing in Publication Data
O'Neill, Maryrose
All about Canadian communities / Maryrose O'Neill.

Includes index.
Contents: [v. 1] Towns — [v. 2] Large cities — [v. 3] Suburban communities — [v. 4] Rural communities — [v. 5] Farming communities — [v. 6] Fishing communities — [v. 7] Forestry communities — [v. 8] Mining communities — [v. 9] Northern communities — [v. 10] Teacher's guide.

ISBN 0-17-620376-1 (v. 1).—ISBN 0-17-620377-X (v. 2).—ISBN 0-17-620378-8 (v. 3).—ISBN 0-17-620379-6 (v. 4).—ISBN 0-17-620384-2 (v. 5).—ISBN 0-17-620380-X (v. 6).—ISBN 0-17-620392-3 (v. 7).—ISBN 0-17-620400-8 (v. 8).—ISBN 0-17-620385-0 (v. 9).—ISBN 0-17-620207-2 (set)

1. Cities and towns—Canada—Juvenile literature. 2. Villages—Canada—Juvenile literature. 3. Community life—Canada—Juvenile literature. I. Title.

HT127.O54 2003   j307'.0971   C2003-900042-7

Table of Contents
(All about what is in the book)

Introduction
(All about beginning the book)

Over 31 million people live in Canada.

Canadians live in big and small communities all across the country.

Canadians live in many different kinds of communities.

In many kinds of communities, people live together in the same place.

A town is one kind of community.

What kind of community do you live in?

An Ontario town's welcome

Description
(All about what towns look like)

Most towns in Canada have more than 1000 people.

Most towns in Canada have more than provides

Each town has its own **government** and have **services**.

Towns clean drinking water, pick up garbage, and make parks. fire departments.

Towns also light streets, build sidewalks, and make parks.

A town has fewer people than a city, but more people than a **rural community**.

What does the picture tell you about life in towns?

Canada

A typical town

Environment
(All about what is in and around a town)

People build a town where they will get what they need to live.

People build a town in a **climate** that will help them survive.

Towns have **natural features** and **built features**.

Many towns are beside natural features, such as rivers, oceans, farmland, forests, or mountains.

People build features such as homes, schools, hospitals, roads, and bridges in towns.

What natural and built features do you see in the photo?

6

The shoreline near Stephenville, Newfoundland

Resources
(All about things towns use)

Every community uses **natural resources, goods,** and services.

Some towns make goods from nearby natural resources, such as farmland, oil fields, and forests.

Towns can make goods, such as food, gas, and paper.

Most towns have services, such as doctors, tours for visitors, and farmers' markets.

Communities trade goods and services with other communities.

What is something your community sells?

Transportation
(All about travelling in and around towns)

In towns, some children walk to school on sidewalks.

In towns, some children walk to school on sidewalks.
In towns, some children walk, cycle, or ride in cars to move around in a town.

People walk, cycle, or ride in cars to move around in a town.

Cars and trucks move goods around in a town.

Townspeople ride in cars, trains, buses, and boats to go to other communities.

Trucks, trains, and boats move goods between towns and other communities.

What kind of transportation do you use?

Inuvik, Northwest Territories

People
(All about who lives in towns)

Some people who live in towns came from other parts of Canada or other countries.

People live, work, go to school, and play in their towns.

People often help each other in towns.

People live closer together in towns than in rural communities.

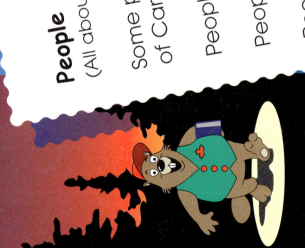

Where do people in your community come from?

12

Children in Inuvik, Northwest Territories

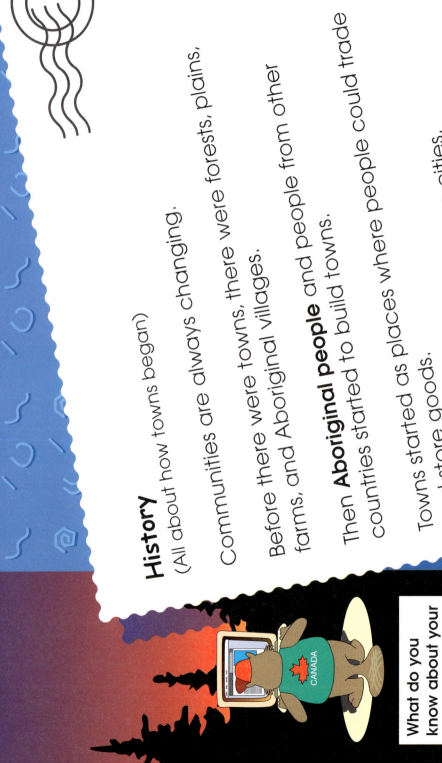

History
(All about how towns began)

Communities are always changing.

Before there were towns, there were forests, plains, farms, and Aboriginal villages.

Then **Aboriginal people** and people from other countries started to build towns.

Towns started as places where people could trade and store goods.

Some towns grew and became cities.

What do you know about your community's history?

Canada

The city of Moncton, New Brunswick, when it was still a town

Occupations
(All about jobs in towns)

People in towns work at different kinds of jobs.

Some people in towns work in small businesses that help townspeople or visitors.

Some people in towns work in stores, gas stations, or offices.

Some people in towns work in government offices.

Some people in towns work in factories, oil fields, schools, hospitals, or fire stations.

Some people in towns work in factories, oil fields, or mines.

What are three jobs in your community?

Firefighters practise in Nackawic, New Brunswick.

NACKAWIC ARENA

Language and Culture
(All about people's languages and traditions)

People in towns can be from many different **cultures**.

People in towns may speak English, French, Aboriginal languages, or languages from other countries.

A town's culture includes its stories, music, and **traditions**.

A town's culture also includes children's clubs and sports teams.

Towns often celebrate their cultures with special days.

What languages do people in your community speak?

A parade in Alberton, Prince Edward Island

Examples of Towns
(All about some Canadian towns)

There are many towns across Canada.

Here are three towns for you to look at.

Lac-Mégantic is a town in Quebec that was built beside a lake and a mountain.

Wainwright is a town in Alberta that was built beside a railway and near farms.

Amherst is a town in Nova Scotia that was built near the Bay of Fundy, which leads to the Atlantic Ocean.

Where is your community located on the map?

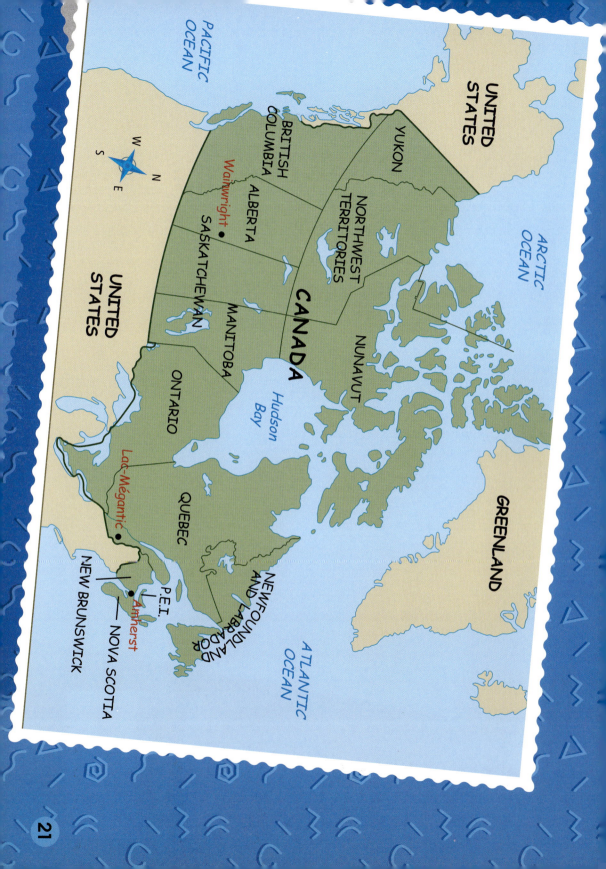

Lac–Mégantic, Quebec

(All about the town of Lac-Mégantic)

The first people to live in the Lac-Mégantic area were the Abenaki, an Aboriginal people.

In the late 1800s, a railroad was built to link it to other communities; Lac-Mégantic became a town in 1907.

Today, about 6000 Canadians live in Lac-Mégantic.

Some people in Lac-Mégantic work at jobs that help visitors who come to see nearby **attractions**.

People in Lac-Mégantic speak French.

What people were first to live in your area?

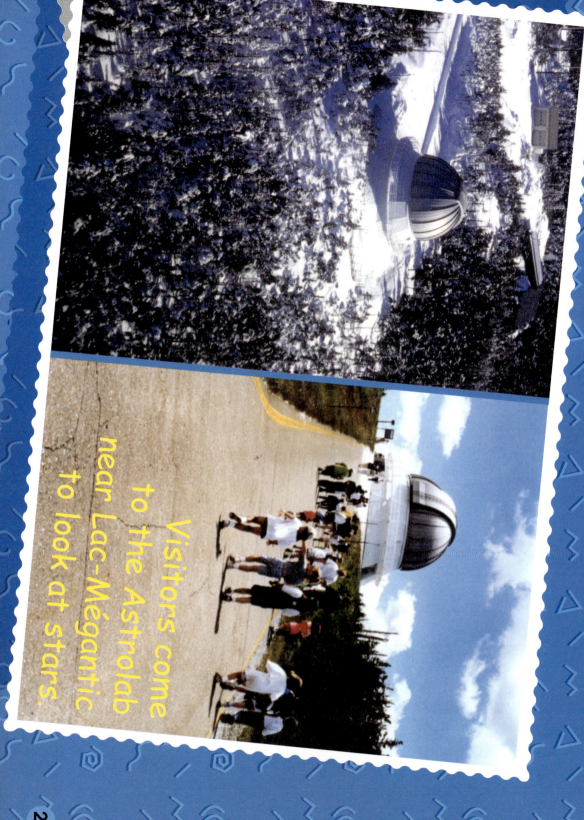

Visitors come to the Astrolab near Lac-Mégantic to look at stars.

Wainwright, Alberta

(All about the town of Wainwright)

Some of the first people to live in the Wainwright area were the Blackfoot, an Aboriginal people.

Wainwright became a town in 1910 when the railway was built nearby.

Today, about 5000 Canadians live in Wainwright.

Some people in Wainwright provide services for nearby farmers, work in the oil and gas fields, or work at the Canadian army training centre.

The plains bison is the **symbol** of Wainwright.

What could be a symbol of your community?

24

A statue of Wainwright's symbol

Amherst, Nova Scotia

(All about the town of Amherst)

Some of the first people to live in the Amherst area were the Mi'kmaq and Malecite, who are Aboriginal peoples.

Amherst became a town in 1889; by 1914 people worked in factories that made railway cars, pianos, and woollen goods.

Today, about 10 000 Canadians live in Amherst.

Some people in Amherst make plastics and batteries.

Nearby farmers use services in Amherst and use trains to move their produce.

How would you travel to Amherst?

26

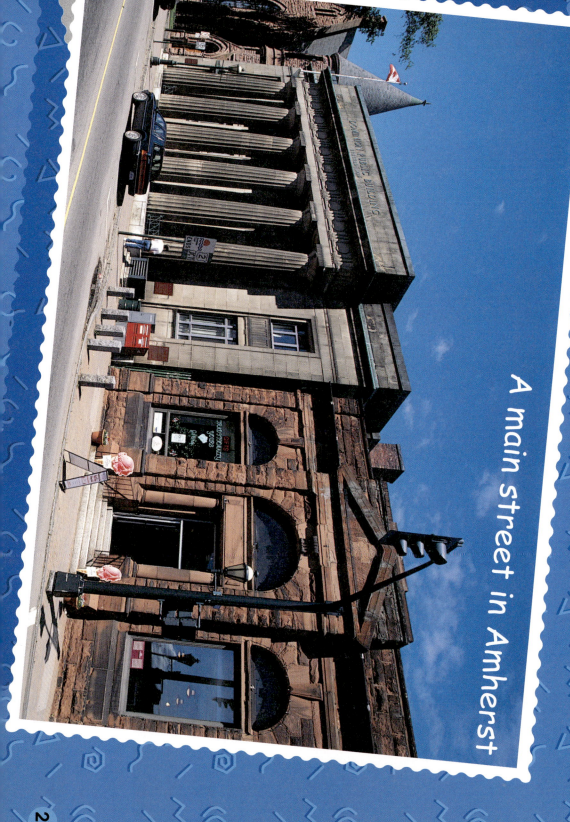

A main street in Amherst

Summary

(All about what the book was about)

Many towns are built beside rivers, lakes, farmland, forests, or mountains.

Each town has its own government.

People in towns work at different kinds of jobs that help townspeople and visitors.

Towns are always changing.

Towns are one of the wonderful kinds of communities found in Canada!

What is wonderful about your community?

28

The town of Osoyoos, British Columbia

Glossary
(All about what the words mean)

Aboriginal peoples (page 14)
Aboriginal peoples are First Nations people, Inuit, and Métis.

attractions (page 22)
Attractions are interesting places or things that people come to see.

built feature (page 6)
A built feature is a part of a community that people make. An example is a road.

climate (page 6)
Climate is the weather patterns of a region, including temperature, rain, and wind patterns.

culture (page 18)
Culture is the arts, beliefs, and traditions that make up people's way of life.

goods (page 8)
Goods are things that people buy and sell.

government (page 4)
A government is a group of people in charge of a town, a province, a country, or another place.

natural feature (page 6)
A natural feature is a part of a community that people have not built. An example is a forest.

natural resource (page 8)
A natural resource is something in nature that people use or sell. An example is fish.

rural community (page 4)
A rural community is a group of people who live in the country.

service (page 4)
A service is an activity that helps people. Often, people pay money for services.

symbol (page 24)
A symbol stands for a person, place, or thing.

traditions (page 18)
Traditions are activities, knowledge, or beliefs that are passed down from older people to younger people.